The Bubble Gum Boy

by

Garry Adams II

AuthorHouse™
1663 Liberty Drive
Bloomington, IN 47403
www.authorhouse.com
Phone: 833-262-8899

*Because of the dynamic nature of the Internet, any web addresses or links contained in
this book may have changed since publication and may no longer be valid. The views
expressed in this work are solely those of the author and do not necessarily reflect the views
of the publisher, and the publisher hereby disclaims any responsibility for them.*

*Any people depicted in stock imagery provided by Getty Images are models,
and such images are being used for illustrative purposes only.
Certain stock imagery © Getty Images.*

This book is printed on acid-free paper.

ISBN: 978-1-4343-7645-9 (sc)

Print information available on the last page.

Published by AuthorHouse 02/21/2023

I would like to thank my son Abel for His infatuation with bubble gum and his desire for me to tell this story over and over again for bed time. "Abel I love you!" and I would like to thank my loving wife who encourages me to finish what I start. "Melanie you complete me."

authorHOUSE

Now Billy got away with chewing bubble gum almost all the time. He would chew bubble gum before school. Billy would chew bubble gum after lunch during recess.

Billy would even chew bubble gum before dinner time while he did home work, and even when he played outside.

One day when Billy was getting dressed for school he could see the bubble gum he chewed the night before.

It was on the bed post, Billy had put it there just before he brushed his teeth and went to bed. "It was put there just last night." Billy said to himself putting his last sock on his foot "It should still taste good its bubble gum."

Billy was all dressed and ready to go down the stairs and have breakfast but he couldn't help but try it. Billy put the bubble gum that was on the bead post into his mouth.

A face appeared on Billy like no other look could possibly look. Chewing on the gum was difficult, it was hard and cold. Not at all what Billy expected. And the taste was gone.

Just then Billy's older sister came into his room. Her hair was red like fire and looked silly bunched together hanging from both sides of her head. "Mom said to hurry up. Your breakfast..."

Sally stopped talking; she noticed Billy's funny expression and asked "What's wrong with you."

"Nothing Really It's just this gum is hard to chew and taste like old bed post" said Billy.

Sally thought for a moment and just like older sisters do. She came up with a solution to the problem. "Just add a piece to the one you already have and that should fix it silly."

And with that Sally went downstairs for breakfast.

Bubble gum was his favorite treat and Billy spent most of his allowance on it. He always kept a lot of bubble gum in his sock drawer.

Getting a piece out. Billy added a piece of bubble gum to the one he already had.

Sally was right! The bubble gum was soft and sweet in his mouth. Billy thought that was a good idea so he stuffed his pocket with bubble gum then went downstairs.

Billy's sister Sally was done eating and leaving the table. Mom said "Drink all your juice Billy." Then Mom went to help fix Sally's hair.

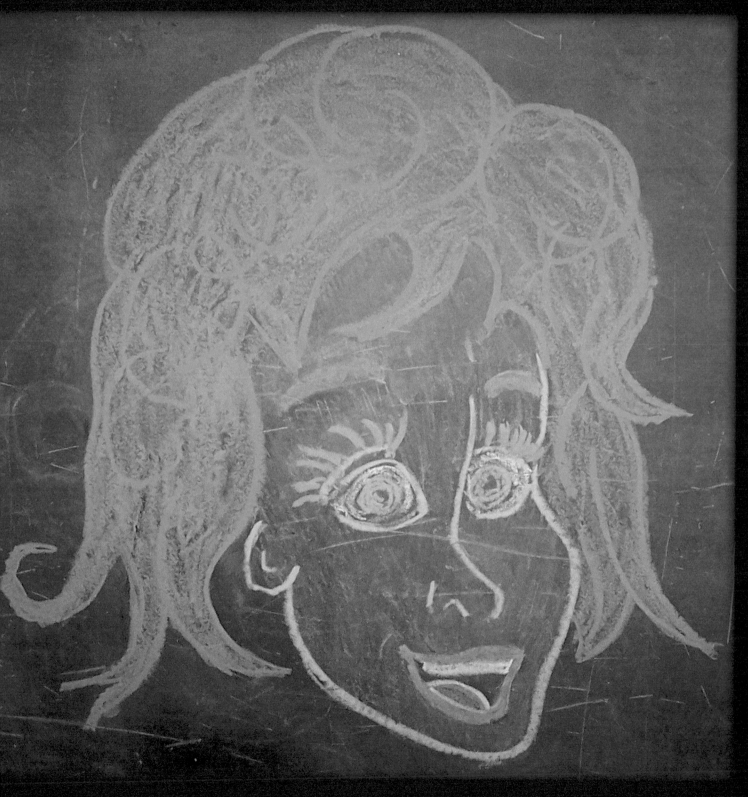

Billy stuck the gum on the side of his plate and ate his breakfast.

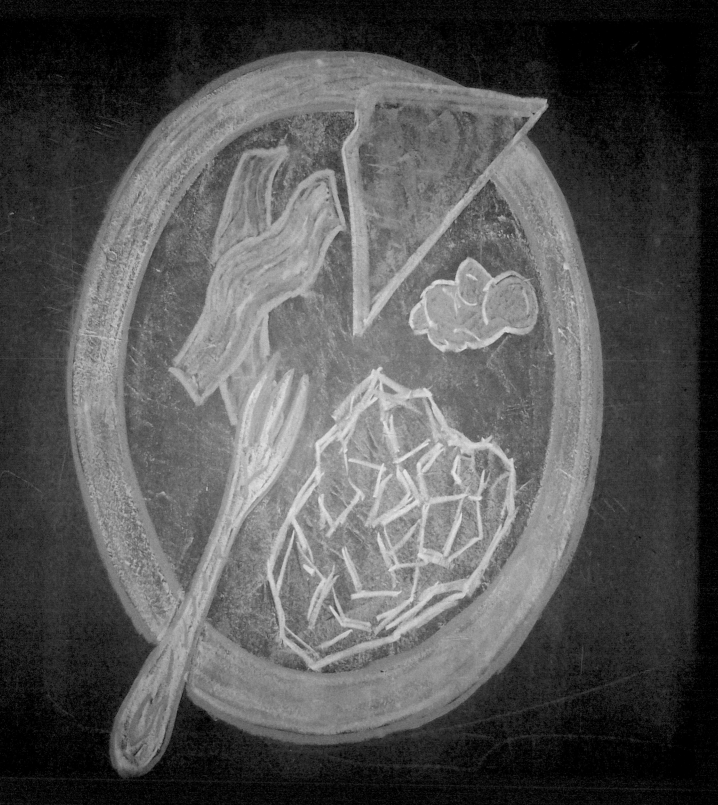

After breakfast Billy washed up and grabbed his jacket, Billy grabbed his book bag, and he grabbed his bubble gum that was on his plate.

Billy ran out the door "Good bye!" He waived at his sister and mother as he headed out for school. Billy stuck the old gum back into his mouth.

When Billy was a little ways down the street he was not happy with the way the bubble gum tastes. Billy thought to his own self "could it have been the orange juice I had at breakfast that made my gum loose its flavor?"

So Billy reached into his pocket and he added a piece of bubble gum to the one he already had into his Mouth. "Mmmm... That is much better." On to school Billy walked.

Billy kept the gum hid in his mouth when he was in class.

During lunch he took the gum out and set it on his sandwich
bag.

After Billy finished his lunch it was time for recess and he put the bubble gum into his mouth but on the playground the bubble gum did not seem to have any flavor and Billy knew what to do!

As Billy was digging in his pocket Tom yelled over to him from the sports shed "You got to hurry if you want a kick ball Billy, the girls are getting them all!"

Billy could not let the girls have all the kick balls. They only took them to keep them from the boys. Billy yelled back "Ige er be righhhh aere!" The gum in his mouth made it difficult to speak, Tom did not understand.

Billy added another piece of bubble gum to the one he already had. "Mmmm...

Munn beh-errr!" Billy thought to his own self. So much gum, So much flavor.

The bell rang and back into class everyone went. Billy kept himself quiet through the rest of the class.

At the end of school Billy was waiting for his friends, they would always walk home together and talk about everything. They mostly talked about the girls at recess. Billy could not talk, only make muffled sounds.

Billy thought his bubble gum was flavorless so... Billy added
a piece of bubble gum to the one he already had. "Mmmm...
Mmmm" The bubble gum was so big, so full of flavor!

Tom asked "Hey Billy Can I have a piece of gum too?" and as
Billy tried to answer him yes "Mm–nnn ahh nnn." Was the only
thing that came out, and tom laughed and laughed.

Billy gave Tom a piece of bubble gum. Tom thought Billy was silly for having all that bubble gum in his mouth. Tom began to think "Hmmm.."

Tom put the gum in his mouth and chewed it until it was soft and then tapped Billy on the shoulder "Can you do this?" and a bubble appeared out of Tom's mouth.

Billy was impressed with his friend's trick and tried to do the same. He blew into the wad of gum and out of his mouth grew a bubble. It grew bigger and bigger then... POP.

Both Tom and Billy walked and blew bubbles on the way home until Billy had a great idea.

There was one piece of bubble gum left in his pocket so☐ Billy added a piece of bubble gum to the one he already had! Billy started to chew and chew.

Tom and Billy stopped walking and other children started to gather around. All were waiting to see what would happen next.

Billy blew a bubble so big he nearly came off the ground and then P O P. All the kids were amazed at the size and encouraged Billy "Do it again. Do it again!" they yelled.

Billy was happy all the kids liked his new trick and he was ready to please his friends blowing big bubbles.

Billy motioned to the kids and Tom said "All right now...give Billy some room everyone, this is going to be the big one!"

Billy blew and he blew. The kids were cheering him on. Billy blew and he blew. The kids cheered even more as the bubble grew and grew.

Billy blew and he blew "Go Billy! Go Billy!" said the kids. Billy blew and he blew.

Up.... Up and away flew Billy The bubble gum boy!

The End

Printed in the United States
by Baker & Taylor Publisher Services